When Dad Showed Me the Universe

Ulf Stark · Eva Eriksson

GECKO PRESS

One day Dad said he thought I was old enough for
him to show me the universe.

"Where is it?" I asked.

"Not too far," he said, taking off his dentist coat with
its flecks of blood.

"Are you going to be warm enough?" my mother asked. "It's pretty cold out there."

"How cold is it at the universe?" I asked.

"Minus 263 degrees," Dad said as he put on his black beret, his leather jacket, and his tall, brown boots.

I put on an extra pair of socks.

Mother hugged us as we left. "Don't be late," she said.

At the gate we turned right. Dad held my hand so I wouldn't get lost.

He took long strides, and he looked at the clouds as he walked. He always did that. When he spoke, white smoke puffed from his mouth.

"It's called steam," said Dad. "It happens because the air in my mouth is warmer than the air outside."

"What actually is the universe?" I asked.

"The entire universe," said Dad, "includes everything, my friend."

The way there was straight ahead and then to the left.

"Is that it?" I asked.

I pointed at the supermarket.

"No," he said. "But we can go in there for our provisions."

"What are provisions?" I asked.

"Things you buy that you need for an expedition," said Dad.

He knew exactly what we needed.

"One packet of gum," he told the shopkeeper.

"Do you need anything else?" she asked. "Because we're about to close for the evening."

"No, that's all," he said.

We walked for a long time.
Past the park where the
toddler pool was closed.

Past the hardware store…

...and past the fish shop, which were both closed as well.
It was starting to get dark.

"Are we there yet?" I asked.

"Are you tired?" asked Dad.

"No, I'm not," I said, although I was.

He whistled so it would be easier for us to keep walking.
The tune floated in a white cloud above his black beret.

Then we came to a ditch full of water.
Dad carried me across so I wouldn't get wet.

"We're almost there," he said.

There were no streetlights at all.

Dad led the way through the grass.

We stopped on a small hill.

"Is this it?"

He nodded. I looked around. I was amazed. I had the feeling I'd been here before, that this was the place where people walked their dogs.

"Let's bring out the provisions," he said. "Here you are."

We stood there chewing solemnly on our gum.

"Can you see?" said Dad.

I could see, even though it was almost dark.

I saw a snail from the universe creeping over a stone.

I saw a blade of grass swaying in the winds of the universe.

There was a flower called a thistle.

And there was Dad, staring at the sky.

"Yes, Dad," I whispered. "I see it."

All of this was the universe!

I thought it was the most beautiful place I'd ever seen.

Then Dad looked at me.

"Don't be silly," he said. "You're supposed to look up."

I looked up. A thousand stars were burning in the sky.

Dad pointed them out. He knew all their names.

"You can see the Little Bear," he said. "And there we have the Serpent, the Horse, and the Scorpion. Do you see its tail?"

I couldn't. For me, the stars all swam together like specks of dust in the living room when the sun shone.

"Yes," I said. Because I didn't want to look silly again.

"Up there, everything is clear and still," he said. "Everything's in its place. See how calm it makes you feel?"

"Mmm," I said.

"That's because it's so big that everything else seems small," he said.

Dad lifted me up so I'd be closer to the stars that were far, far away.

"Some of them don't even exist," he said. "They've gone out already."

"But we can still see them," I said.

"Yes, we can see their light," said Dad. "It may take several hundred years to arrive here."

I looked at the stars that weren't there.

And Dad went on telling me their names and carrying me.

"The Swan," he said. "The Harp. Big Dog."

Then he was quiet. His nostrils flared.

"What on earth is that?" he said.

"What?" I asked.

"What's that stink?" he snorted.

I knew. I knew what he'd stepped in.
"It's Big Dog!" I said.

Then we went home. Dad had lost his enthusiasm.
He looked at the boot he'd wiped in the grass.

"You're probably too little anyway," he said.

Then he walked in silence for a bit.

"All I wanted was to show you something beautiful that
you'd remember forever," he said, taking my hand.

"But I will," I said.

When we got home, we had sandwiches and hot chocolate.

"So, how was the universe?" asked my mother.

"It was beautiful," I said. "And funny."

This edition first published in 2015 by Gecko Press
PO Box 9335, Marion Square, Wellington 6141, New Zealand
info@geckopress.com

English language edition © Gecko Press Ltd 2015

First American edition published in 2015 by Gecko Press USA, an imprint of Gecko Press Ltd.
A catalog record for this book is available from the US Library of Congress.
Distributed in the United States and Canada by Lerner Publishing Group,
www.lernerbooks.com

Distributed in the United Kingdom by Bounce Sales and Marketing,
www.bouncemarketing.co.uk

Distributed in Australia by Scholastic Australia,
www.scholastic.com.au

Distributed in New Zealand by Random House NZ,
www.randomhouse.co.nz
A catalogue record for this book is available from the National Library of New Zealand

First published by Bonnier Carlsen, Stockholm, Sweden
Published in the English language by arrangement with Bonnier Rights, Stockholm, Sweden
Original title: *När pappa visade mig världsalltet*
Text © Ulf Nilsson 1998
Illustrations © Eva Eriksson 1998

The cost of this translation was defrayed by a subsidy from the Swedish Arts Council,
gratefully acknowledged.

Translated by Julia Marshall
Edited by Penelope Todd
Typesetting by Luke & Vida Kelly, New Zealand
Printed in China by Everbest Printing Co Ltd, an accredited ISO 14001 & FSC certified printer

Hardback ISBN: 978-1-927271-81-0
Paperback ISBN: 978-1-927271-82-7
E-book available

For more curiously good books, visit www.geckopress.com